SNOW ON SNOW ON SNOW

Cheryl Chapman

paintings by Synthia Saint James

Scholastic Inc.
New York   Toronto   London   Auckland   Sydney

With thanks to Pierce Pettis

ISBN 0-590-73097-5

12 11 10 9 8 7 6 5 4 3 2 1   6 7 8 9/9 0 1/0

Printed in the U.S.A.   14

First Scholastic printing, February 1996

In the bleak midwinter,
    Frosty wind made moan,
Earth stood hard as iron,
    Water like a stone;
Snow had fallen, snow on snow,
    Snow on snow,
In the bleak midwinter,
    Long ago.

from "In the Bleak Midwinter"
by Christina Rossetti (1830–1894)

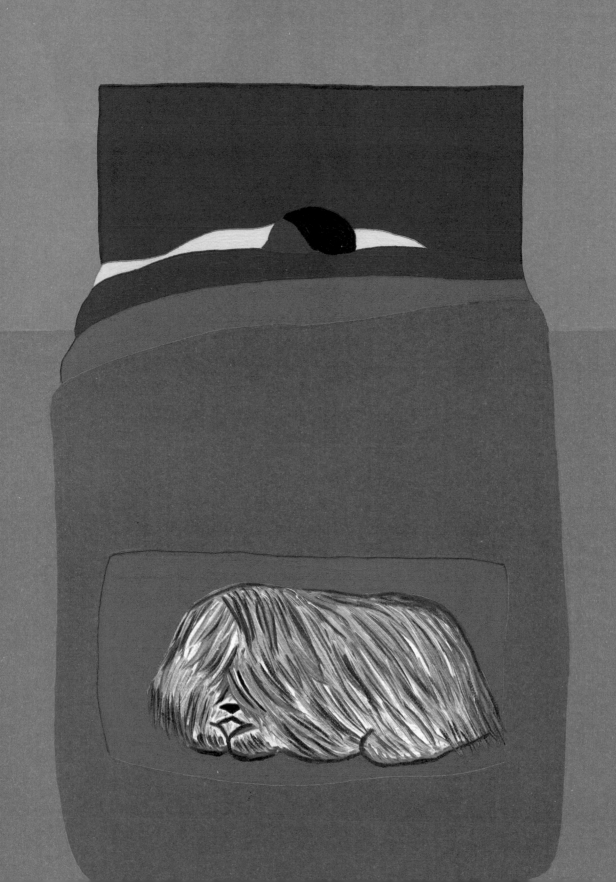

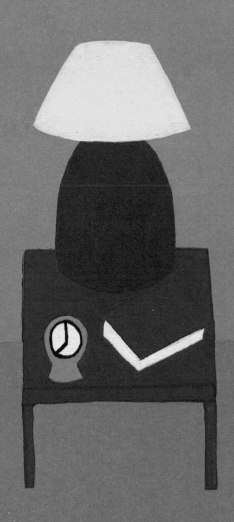

**Once upon a winter's day
I woke up
under blankets under blankets under blankets.**

At breakfast
Mama filled up my plate
with food next to food next to food.

I pulled on
clothes over clothes over clothes.

**We stepped out the door
into snow on snow on snow.**

**We climbed
up the hill up the hill up the hill
and found our friends...**

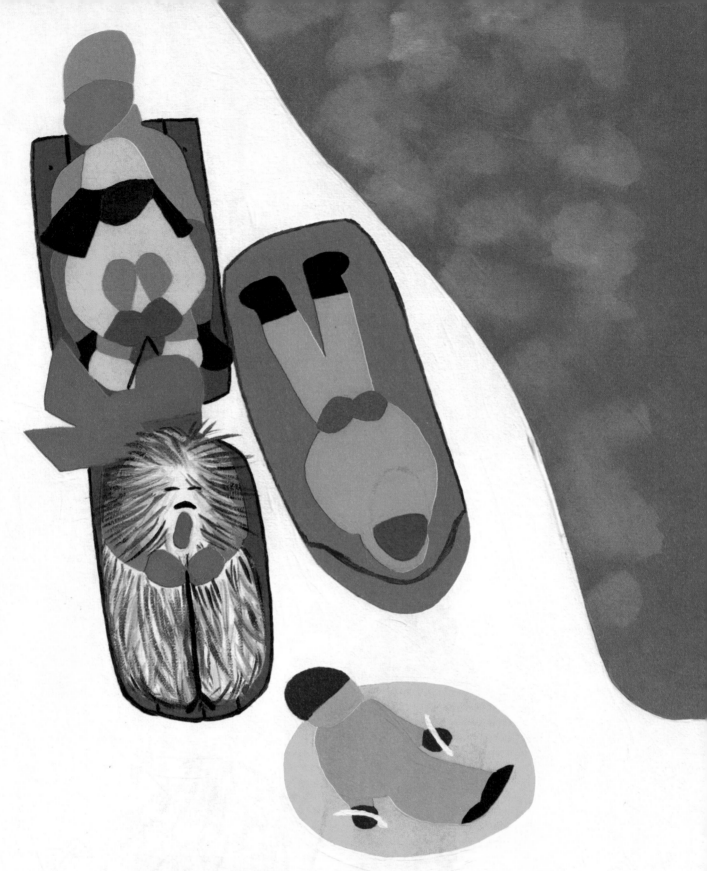

on sleds beside sleds beside sleds.

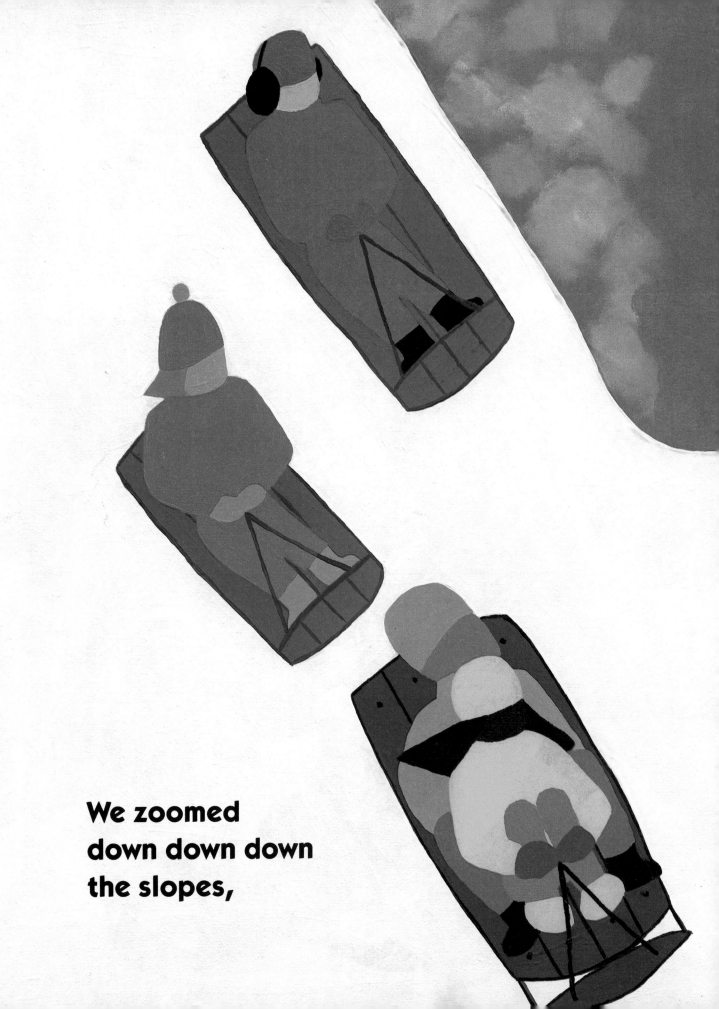

We zoomed
down down down
the slopes,

spinning out at the end.

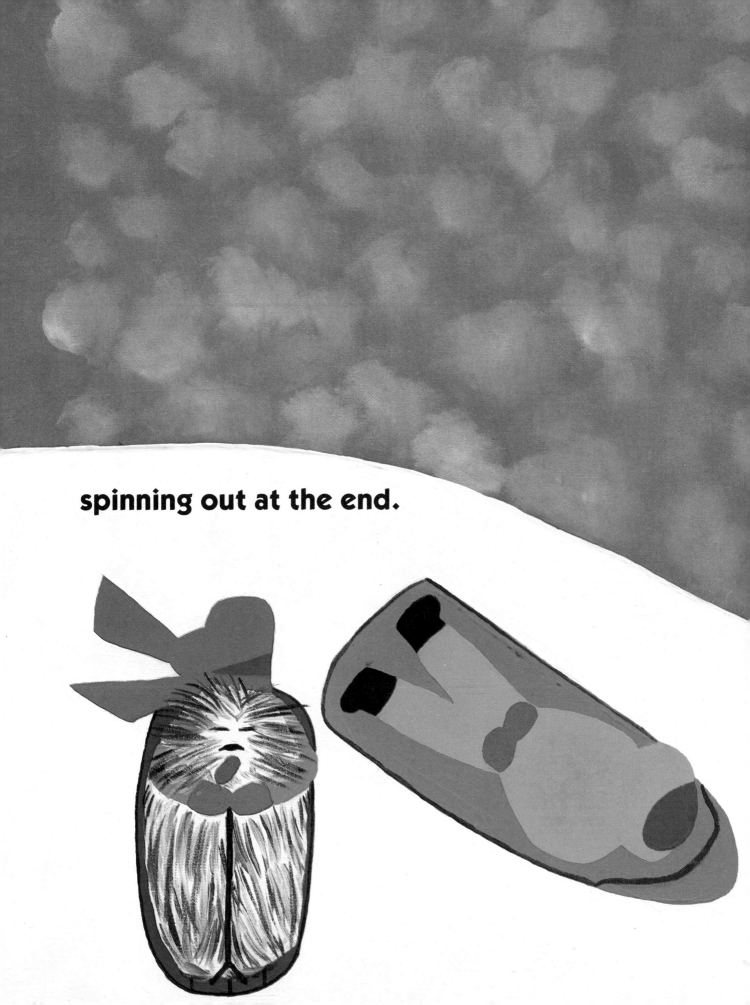

But where did Clancy go?

behind trees.

We searched
around bushes
around thickets
around cattails.

Clancy had disappeared
into the snow
into the wind
into the air.

**Tears on tears on tears
froze my face.**

**Below drifts below drifts below drifts
of snow
there came a woof.**

**And
we all lived
happily
ever after ever after ever after.**